I LOVE MY
Thick Curly Hair

Ajiri Edojah

For My Daughter Kessi.

Copyright © 2022 Ajiri Edojah

All rights reserved. No part of this publication may be reproduced, distributed, or transmitted in any form or by any means, including photocopying, recording, or other electronic or mechanical methods, without the prior written permission of the publisher, except in the case of brief quotations embodied in critical reviews and certain other noncommercial uses permitted by copyright law. For permission requests, write to the publisher, addressed "Attention: Permissions Coordinator," at the address below.

Hardcover ISBN: 978-1-63616-087-0

Published & Illustarted By Opportune Independent Publishing Company

There once was a little girl
with thick curly hair.

Every morning as her mother brushed her hair she screamed, "I hate my curly hair. I don't like it at all. I wish it were straight like yours instead of all these curls."

That evening, the little girl's mother thought about what her daughter said. "I want our daughter to be proud of who she is and to know that her curly hair is beautiful," she said to her husband.

Her husband looked at her and said, "How can she be proud when the only image of beauty she sees are of women with straight hair…like yours."

The little girl's mother gasped as she looked at herself in the mirror. Her daughter had never seen her thick curly hair that she hides under her wigs.

The next morning, the little girl's mother woke up with a plan. She removed her wig and let her thick curly hair down. She pulled out a magazine titled Black Queens and began flipping through the pages.

When the little girl came down for breakfast, she was shocked to see her mother's hair. "Mommy look at your hair," she screamed. "It looks just like mine! I never knew it was curly all this time."

The little girl's mother pulled her daughter close and said, baby, this is me...the real me. My hair is thick and curly underneath my wigs.

"I know all the princesses you see on tv have straight hair, but do not set your eyes on them for you are more than a princess, you are a queen."

She began showing her daughter pictures of beautiful black queens with thick curly hair like hers.

From that day forward the little girl began to love her thick curly hair.

Every morning she looks in the mirror and says "I am a black queen and my thick curly hair is my crown! I will wear it proudly."

Printed in the USA
CPSIA information can be obtained
at www.ICGtesting.com
LVHW061949141223
766501LV00016B/139